Printed in the United States of America

First Edition

1 3 5 7 9 10 8 6 4 2

Library of Congress Catalog Card Number on file.

ISBN: 0-7868-3502-8

Visit www.disneybooks.com

By Princess Aurora

As told to Kiki Thorpe
Illustrated by the Disney Storybook Artists

Disney
PRESS

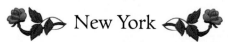 New York

1

Briar Rose

I didn't like my name. I never did. It sounded so—well, *simple*. "Briar Rose," I imagined people saying with a chuckle. "Just sprinkle water on her head, and flowers will grow out her ears!" It made me mad just thinking about it.

I may have grown up in the woods, but I'm no country bumpkin. I'm a lot smarter than folks might think.

There was that morning, for instance, when my aunts asked me to go berry picking.

"We need berries," Aunt Merryweather declared, clear out of the blue. She picked up a basket and pushed it into my hands.

"Yes, er, lots and lots of berries," Aunt Fauna agreed. "We're, um, going to make blackberry jam! That's right. A whole barrelful!"

Well, I saw right through their game. The day before, I had picked berries until my fingers turned purple. If you looked in our cellar, you would have found enough blackberries to give a bear a bellyache! So I knew they were just trying to get me out of the house.

But for the life of me I couldn't think why! After all, it was my sixteenth birthday. You'd think they would do something nice, like throw a little party. Or at least sing "Happy Birthday."

But they just hustled me out of the cottage, then stood there in the doorway, waving good-bye.

"Now, don't hurry back," Aunt Flora said.

"But don't go too far," Aunt Merryweather chimed in.

"And don't speak to any strangers," Aunt Flora added. She always said the same thing when I left the house.

I'd lived with my aunts in the old woodcutter's cottage ever since I was a tiny baby. (Aunt Flora says they found me in the garden under a cabbage leaf. Of course, she's just pulling my leg. I know the stork brought me, just like everyone else.) They are dear, sweet women, like mothers to me. But they could be just a teensy bit strict.

Like that rule about strangers. If I ever met someone I didn't know in the forest, I was to turn around and walk straight home, without so much as a "howdy-do." Aunt Flora said there were hideous goblins nearby, and wicked fairies who wanted to do me harm. But I'm no dummy. I knew what they were really afraid of.

They were afraid I'd meet a *boy*.

Well, I thought, they didn't have to worry about that. I had searched every nook and cranny of that forest, and if there was one thing I was sure about, it was this: there were no boys in those woods.

2

That Special Someone

As I walked toward my favorite blackberry patch, swinging my berry basket, sweet little songbirds circled my head, twittering cheerfully. Bunny rabbits hopped along at my heels, and an owl hooted at me from the trees.

What could be better than sunshine, fresh air, and a walk in the woods with my little forest friends? I thought. Then I noticed something strange.

All the rabbits were hopping along in pairs.

I looked around. The squirrels were snuggling. The chipmunks were cuddling. Even the quail looked as cozy as lovebirds. Everyone in the forest had found a special someone.

Everyone, that is, except for me.

With a heavy sigh, I sat down on a mossy rock. Would I ever leave this deep, dark forest? I wondered. Would I ever meet my own special someone?

"Why do they still treat me like a child?" I pondered aloud.

"Who?" the owl hooted. I was glad he asked.

"Aunts Flora and Fauna and Merryweather," I explained. "They never want me to meet anyone."

The animals gathered around me, emitting concerned squeaks. A chipmunk nudged my ankle. The quail cooed sympathetically. Now, Rose, they seemed to say, don't be sad. Think of the berry basket as half full, not half empty!

They're right, I told myself. After all, I was young and healthy. I had an entire forest full of cute and cuddly friends. And what's more, I *did* have someone special.

That's when I let the animals in on a little secret.

"But I've fooled my aunts," I told them. "I *have* met someone."

The sparrows tittered. The squirrels pricked up their ears. Those little animals just love gossip.

"Who?" the owl wanted to know.

So I told them all about a prince I knew. "He's tall and handsome and *soooo* romantic," I gushed. "We walk together and talk together. And just before we say good-bye, he takes me in his arms, and then . . ."

I paused. The animals leaned forward, winking their beady little eyes. It was so quiet, you could have heard a pine needle drop.

"And then I wake up," I finished. There were squeals and squawks of disappointment. "Yes, it's only in my dreams," I confessed. "But they say if you dream a thing more than once, it's sure to come true."

The owl slowly blinked. The rabbits wiggled their little noses skeptically.

"Oh, I don't believe it, either," I assured them. "I should think you have to dream a thing nine or ten times before it comes true. But you know, I'm already up to eight!"

And then I closed my eyes and recalled my dream prince. He had twinkling eyes and a kind smile and his hair was soft as silk. He took me in his arms and looked into my eyes, then he leaned forward and . . .

Thump.

My eyes flew open. Was it my imagination, or had I heard the sound of a footstep?

Thump.

There it was again! I looked around and gasped as . . .

A stranger stepped out of the bushes.

3

The Man of My Dreams

He wore soft leather boots and a flowing cloak made of fine red wool. A dashing felt hat sat at a rakish angle on his head. And he walked with a funny hop in his step.

I was certain I'd never seen him before. Yet when I peered beneath the brim of his hat, his sharp eyes seemed familiar. And I thought I recognized his beaky nose. . . .

"Who?" the stranger asked.

It was the owl dressed up in a cloak and hat! Two little birds held up the edges of his cloak, as if a pair of shoulders sat beneath it. Below, on the ground, two rabbits hopped up and down inside a pair of boots, as if they were dancing a jig.

"Why, it's my dream prince!" I cried, pretending to be astonished.

The owl dipped his head, bowing to me. I curtsied back. Then, grabbing him by the collar, I began to sing and waltz through the woods, just as if he really was my dream prince.

And then it happened.

As I twirled around an oak tree, singing a high note, the owl suddenly joined in on harmony.

My, that owl has a nice tenor voice, I thought.

And then I thought, owls can't sing!

I whirled around.

There, standing right in front of me, was a tall young man. And was he ever a mess! His clothes were muddy and his hair was full of leaves. Yet his brown eyes shone like agates. And when he smiled, his dimples looked deep enough to plant corn in.

I was so startled, I nearly tumbled into a blackberry bush.

"I'm sorry," he said. "I didn't mean to frighten you."

"It wasn't that," I said, feeling flustered. "It's just that you're—" Awfully cute, I was thinking.

"A stranger?" he said.

That too, I thought. Suddenly all my aunts' warnings about strangers flashed into my head.

But they flashed right out again a second later, because the young man took my hand, and before I knew what was happening, I was waltzing through the forest in his arms.

And do you know what? He was an excellent dancer!

As we waltzed through the glade, I asked him what he was doing in the forest.

"I was just riding by," he told me. "I'm a prince from the next kingdom over."

I looked at his messy hair and muddy clothes. He couldn't fool me. "Ha-ha," I replied. "And I'm a princess!"

We both got a good laugh out of that one.

We stopped to rest on a shady overlook. Somehow his arm slipped around my back and my head ended up on his shoulder.

"Who are you? What's your name?" he murmured into my hair.

"My name? Oh, it's Bri—" I began. Then I reconsidered. What if he thought I was just some country bumpkin?

I decided it would be better to remain a bit mysterious.

"I—I can't tell you," I said. Grabbing my basket and shawl, I sprang to my feet and began to run back through the trees.

"But when will I see you again?" the young man called after me.

"Oh, never! Never!" I cried.

Then again, maybe "never" was a bit *too* mysterious.

"On second thought, this evening!" I called back over my shoulder. "Come to the cottage in the glen."

And with my heart hopping like a bunny rabbit, I ran home.

4

Surprise!

It was late afternoon by the time I reached the cottage, and my basket didn't have enough berries for one single muffin, let alone a whole barrelful of blackberry jam.

Would my aunts be angry? I didn't know. I didn't care. I knew that as soon as they saw what a sweet, handsome, well-mannered young man I'd plucked out of the bushes, they'd be very pleased.

But when I opened the door, the cottage was dark.

"Hello?" I called. "Where is everybody?"

Then my heart nearly jumped out of my chest for the second time that day. For on the kitchen table sat a towering pink-and-blue birthday cake, with sixteen candles flickering on top. And next to it, draped over a chair, was a brand-new blue dress in exactly my size.

"Surprise! Surprise! Surprise!" my aunts cried, leaping out from behind the stairwell.

I should have known then that something was wrong. My aunts are the sweetest women in the world, but they can't cook or clean or darn a sock to save their lives. And I knew for certain no bakeries delivered to our neck of the woods.

But at that moment my mind was on other things.

"Oh, my dears," I said, giving each of them a hug. "This is the happiest day of my life! Just wait till you meet him."

The gale force of their gasps could have knocked down a small forest.

"Him?"

"Rose!"

"You've met some *stranger*?"

"Actually, he's a very old friend," I hastily explained. "We met ages ago . . . once upon a dream."

Aunt Flora bit her lip. Aunt Fauna wrung her hands. Aunt Merryweather looked like she might cry. I could see they weren't buying that argument.

"And, er, anyway, I *am* sixteen," I quickly added.

Then I got my second birthday surprise of the day: my aunts told me I was already betrothed.

"Betrothed?" I hollered. I'd always known my aunts were strict about boys, but this was really going too far!

"To Prince Phillip, dear," Aunt Fauna said.

Well, I may have been a hillbilly, but I was no fool. I wasn't falling for that one. "But to marry a prince," I pointed out, "I'd have to be . . ."

"A princess," Aunt Merryweather said with a nod.

"And you are, dear," Aunt Fauna added.

"Princess Aurora," Aunt Flora said, and the look on her face told me she was not pulling my leg this time.

This was very bad news. I may have lived deep in the forest, but I wasn't totally in the dark. Everyone in the kingdom knew about Aurora, the poor princess who had been cursed by an evil fairy. Rumor had it that any day now she would prick her finger on a spindle (whatever that was) . . . and die!

Not that I believed in fairies. Still, "cursed" is not exactly the sort of reputation a girl wants to go around with.

"No, thanks," I told Aunt Flora. "I'll pass. Give the job to someone else."

But Aunt Flora was firm. "Tonight we're taking you back to your father, King Stefan," she said.

"But, I can't go!" I cried. "He's coming here tonight. It's our first date!"

"I'm sorry," Aunt Flora replied, shaking her head sadly. "But you must never see that young man again."

5

Ouch

So *this* is the inside of a castle, I thought. It looks much bigger from the outside.

Still, I couldn't help gawking a little. Silk carpets covered the castle floors and elaborate tapestries hung from the walls. The rooms were filled with all sorts of fine things: gilt mirrors and antique vases, oil paintings and marble statues. There was even an indoor toilet! I thought the king and queen must own everything but the moon.

My aunts led me into a room as big as our whole cottage. A huge fire popped and crackled in the hearth. As Aunt Flora settled me on a velvet cushion, Merryweather bolted the door behind us and Fauna shut the drapes tightly.

"And now," said Aunt Flora somberly, "the crowning touch." Pulling a thin wand from her sleeve, she waved it over my head, and suddenly a golden crown appeared! Right out of thin air! She placed it on my head.

Well! I thought, looking at my reflection in a mirror. Wouldn't the chipmunks get a kick out of that!

But thinking of the chipmunks reminded me of the forest. And the forest reminded me of the cottage. And that reminded me of the cute, messy boy, who was probably waiting for me this very minute.

I started to sniffle again.

"Now, dear. Don't cry," Aunt Fauna said. Which only made me cry harder. I put my head down on my arms and bawled like a billy goat.

"Let her have a few minutes alone," I heard Aunt Flora say. Then their little footsteps pattered across the floor and the door closed shut behind them.

Suddenly the room felt cold. Lifting my head, I saw that the fire had gone out. A few thin wisps of smoke curled from the cinders.

As I watched, the smoke turned green. Suddenly, within the smog, a glowing orb appeared. The orb floated in the air, heavy and green, like an apple without a tree.

Now I was curious! Wiping my eyes on my sleeve, I walked over to the hearth and peered inside. The hearthstones shimmered, then vanished—right before my eyes! In their place was a long, winding staircase.

Fancy that, I thought. A staircase in the hearth. What won't these royal types think of next?

The little green orb bounced in the air. "Let's go!" it seemed to say. So, gathering my skirt in my hands, I followed it up the stairs.

Up, up, up I climbed. It seemed like I might climb all the way to the moon! I started to wonder if the king and queen actually owned that too.

But the staircase didn't lead to the moon. It led to a small, round room, high at the top of a tower. The green orb hovered in the center, then with a sudden *poof!* it vanished. In its place stood the oddest piece of machinery I had ever seen.

It had four legs and a big wooden wheel. At one end there was a thingamabob wrapped in wool, which stuck straight up in the air. The tip of it looked very sharp.

Just then I noticed a tall, thin woman standing in the corner of the room. She was elegantly dressed in a long, black gown, but her skin looked rather, well, *green*. She looked like she could use some fresh air and exercise.

"Go on," she said. "Touch the spindle."

"So *that's* what a spindle is!" I exclaimed. "I always wondered." And without thinking, I reached out my hand.

Well, it *was* very sharp. As I looked at the drop of blood welling on the tip of my finger, my last thought was, "Princess Aurora" *does* have a nice ring to it. . . .

And then everything went black.

6

The Man of My Dreams, Part 2

My dream prince was tall and handsome and *soooo* romantic. He had twinkling eyes and a kind smile and his hair—well, his hair was full of leaves! And his clothes were damp and muddy! But I didn't mind. He took me in his arms, and looked into my eyes, then he leaned forward and . . . he kissed me!

My eyes flew open. The cute, messy boy from the woods was standing over me. His hair was sweaty and his clothes were torn and rumpled. He smelled like a horse. But his brown eyes shone like moonlight, and his dimples looked deep enough to mine for gold.

What a pity that I have to marry a prince, I thought.

"I hate to break this to you," I whispered. "But I'm already engaged."

But the boy just smiled and kissed me again. Then he took my hand and led me down that long, long staircase.

As soon as we reached the bottom, everything became very confusing. A roomful of people in fancy clothing was staring at us and clapping. An elegant man and woman wearing crowns rushed forward to embrace me. These must be my parents, I thought. Then who is that fat little man in the crown over there? And why is everyone so happy to see this peasant boy from the woods?

But when people started calling him "Prince Phillip," I put two and two together. The boy from the woods really *was* a prince—my dream prince! And I'd been right all along! You *do* have to dream a thing more than once before it comes true. (You have to dream it nine times, to be exact.) Like I said, I'm smarter than people might think.

Phillip and I got married right away and moved into a great big castle built by his father, King Hubert (the fat little man in the crown). No one calls me Briar Rose anymore. These days my name is Princess Aurora, but I tell most people to just call me "Princess." It sounds so—royal.

Phillip and I have had a great time getting to know each other better. He's always making up funny stories. For instance, the way he tells it, he fought through a forest of magic thorns and battled a fire-breathing dragon—all just to kiss me!

"Ha-ha," I say. "And that goose we just bought lays golden eggs."

He is such a kidder.

My Side
of the Story

By Maleficent

As told to Kiki Thorpe
Illustrated by the Disney Storybook Artists

1

Success

There are three rules of thumb that I always follow:

1) *Always return an insult with generosity.*
2) *Never hold a grudge.*
3) *Do unto others as you would have them do unto you.*

These three simple rules are the key to a rich and rewarding life. And I should know. Until my recent troubles, I was the most successful businesswoman this side of Kingdom Come.

Enchantment Value Industries Limited—that's my corporation (E.V.I.L. for short). Maybe you've heard of it? We specialize in black magi—I mean, *market*—enterprise. And I can proudly say we have branches all over the world.

But my success has come at a price. Over the years I've been the victim of a lot of vicious gossip. People say I'm a ruthless witch (I simply know what I want). They say I lead a gang of hideous goblins (my company maintains a strict policy of nondiscrimination). And, they say a storm of wrath and frustration continually thunders around my castle in the Forbidden Mountains (it may be a bit rainy, but I got an incredible bargain on real estate!). Really, it's amazing what people will say to drag a good, hardworking woman's name through the mud.

But the ugliest rumor I ever heard was that I placed a curse on Princess Aurora. Complete and utter nonsense!

I'll admit I've never been close to the royal family. Aurora's meddling father, King Stefan, has been the fly in my bubbling brew since the day I opened my company's door.

But I've always had a soft spot for the princess. The fact is, I felt sorry for her. And when you hear *my* side of the story you'll know the truth: I've gone out of my way to help her since the day she was born.

2

A Generous Offer

I was out of town visiting my poultry ranch—we breed a rare variety of golden-egg-laying geese—when I heard that King Stefan and his queen had given birth to a baby girl.

I, myself, am not a family-oriented person (my work keeps me much too busy). But I was very pleased for the king and queen. When I heard there would be a baby shower, I rushed back home immediately to offer my congratulations.

Imagine my surprise when, upon arriving at my headquarters, I found the mailbox empty. Could it be that the king and queen had failed to send me an invitation? *Me*, the founder and CEO of one of the largest corporations in the world?

Don't be silly, I told myself. Surely it was an oversight. After all, Their Highnesses had an entire kingdom to invite. Brushing the thought from my mind like a cobweb, I donned my best black dress and set off for the palace.

Well, you wouldn't believe the scene that greeted my eyes. Every second duke and third earl in the land had turned up for the party. It was a zoo! I had to elbow my way through the crowd just to get in.

I arrived in the throne room just in time to see my three least favorite fairies in the world: Flora, Fauna, and Merryweather. Ever since the king put those noodleheads in charge of his "Pretty Our City" program, they've taken themselves much too seriously. They're always flitting around the kingdom, turning ravens into bluebirds and toadstools into tulips. (As if ravens and toadstools aren't perfectly nice to begin with!)

Everyone in the room watched as Flora approached the cradle.

"Little princess," she said to the sleeping baby. "My gift shall be the gift of beauty."

"Oooh!" the crowd exclaimed.

As if that wasn't silly enough, Fauna stepped forward next.

"Tiny princess, my gift shall be the gift of song," she said.

"Ahhh!" everyone sighed.

Fools! I thought. I've been around long enough to know that you can't get by on a pretty face and a nice singing voice. Common sense and a good work ethic, that's what a girl needs in this day and age.

Suddenly, I had a brilliant idea.

I could offer the princess a job! It just so happens that I own several textile mills in the kingdom (we specialize in spinning straw into gold). An internship at the factory would teach her a skill, as well as provide some valuable lessons about hard work.

Eager to share this splendid plan, I approached the king and queen.

I admit, they did not look very happy to see me. Ever since the king shut down my Poison Apple-of-the-Month mail-order business, there has been some tension between us. Still, I thought we could put aside our differences on this happy day.

"This is quite a party, King Stefan," I began. "I felt truly distressed at not receiving an invitation."

But before the king had a chance to apologize, that little busybody Merryweather butted in.

"You weren't wanted!" she said rudely.

"Not wanted?" I gasped. "Oh, dear."

It was a dreadfully awkward moment.

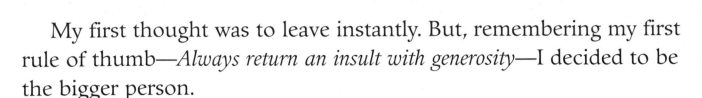

My first thought was to leave instantly. But, remembering my first rule of thumb—*Always return an insult with generosity*—I decided to be the bigger person.

I offered the princess the job anyway.

"She could start before the sun sets on her sixteenth birthday," I explained. "And not a day sooner." I have always been scrupulous about child labor laws.

But rather than thank me for my generous offer, the king turned red with rage.

"The princess? In a textile mill?" he roared. "Are you mad? That's preposterous!"

My next statement I have lived to regret.

"What are you afraid of?" I snapped at the king. "That she will prick her finger on the spindle of a spinning wheel and *die*?"

I'm afraid my sarcasm was misunderstood.

The king rose from his throne. "Seize that creature!" he bellowed. His guards rushed toward me.

"Never mind," I said, shaking off their hands. "I'll show myself out."

Some people are so ungrateful.

No Hard Feelings
(or Rule Number Two)

But my troubles didn't end there.

That very same day, King Stefan issued a decree: every spinning wheel in the kingdom was to be destroyed! His soldiers turned the kingdom inside out. They piled every spinning wheel they found into a huge, crackling bonfire that lit up the night.

Of course, this made things a tad difficult for my textile business. And it plunged the entire kingdom into a terrible fashion crisis!

I didn't see the princess again for sixteen years. I don't remember where I heard she was living in the old woodcutter's cottage in the forest. Some little birdie told me, I guess. It's not as if it was a secret. In fact, the whole kingdom was talking about the princess. Recently some ugly rumors had started to spread. People were saying that I'd made an evil prophecy, that on the very day Princess Aurora turned sixteen she would prick her finger on a spindle . . . and die.

I realized it was time to clear the air. Now, the royal family had not been kind to me. But my second rule of thumb is *Never hold a grudge*.

When I heard the king and queen were throwing a sweet sixteen party for the princess that very evening, I was delighted. This would be the perfect chance to patch things up with the royal family.

I decided to pay the princess a friendly visit.

A Plea for Help

I would like to clear up some nasty lies about my visit with Princess Aurora that day. To begin with, I did *not* change myself into a wisp of smoke and steal into King Stefan's castle. Such nonsense! I simply walked past the guards dozing at the gate. Is it my fault the palace has lousy security?

I found the princess in a bedroom high at the top of a tower. She had indeed grown into a lovely young woman, with long golden hair and full red lips. But her smooth cheeks were streaked with tears.

And no wonder! She was wearing a frightfully unstylish dress in a hideous periwinkle color. It nearly made me cry, too!

"There, there," I said soothingly. "I have a stunning black cocktail dress you can borrow for the party. I'm sure it will fit you perfectly."

The princess broke into fresh sobs.

"It's not that!" she wailed. "My life is ruined! I finally met the man of my dreams, and now I have to marry a horrible prince!"

I made her take deep breaths until she was calm enough to explain. It seems that on one of her nature walks, Aurora had fallen in love with a peasant boy, only to find out she was already betrothed to the son of King Hubert, her father's old golfing buddy.

Tears streaming down her face, the princess begged me for help.

Normally I do not do charity work. But I remembered my third rule of thumb: *Do unto others as you would have them do unto you.* I asked myself, "If I was in the princess's pitiful periwinkle shoes, would I want a clever person like myself to step in and save the day?"

The answer was simple. Yes, I would.

"Why not pretend to be dead?" I suggested, thinking quickly. "This will surely discourage the annoying prince. Once he's gone, you'll be free to marry anyone you please!"

Princess Aurora was delighted with this plan, and we promptly put it into action.

For the record, I never saw a spindle, a spinning wheel, or even so much as a loose thread in that room. It's true that I helped the princess fall into a deathlike slumber, but only with a perfectly safe, all-natural sleep aid. I gave her exactly two tablets—no more, no less—which is the recommended dosage for adults.

The sun had just dipped below the horizon as she settled down for her nap. She carefully arranged her dress and fanned her shining hair out across the pillow. Before she closed her eyes, she asked for one last favor.

"Would you mind meeting my true love at the woodcutter's cottage?" she pleaded. "Just explain to him what has happened."

I was tempted to refuse. I had done enough good deeds for one day.

But before I could say no, the princess was asleep.

5

The Prince

There was a rap at the cottage door.

"Come in," I said.

The door swung open and a young man stepped into the room. He wore a red hat and a dashing cashmere cloak. I immediately recognized him as Prince Phillip, King Hubert's son.

"What a pleasant surprise!" I exclaimed. "I was expecting a peasant, and lo—I meet a prince instead!" And not just any prince. Prince Phillip, the very person Princess Aurora was engaged to marry!

"What are you doing here?" he asked. "Where's that cute country bumpkin I met in the woods?"

Then it dawned on me: Prince Phillip was the young man Aurora had mistaken for a peasant boy. And by some charming twist of fate, he had mistaken Princess Aurora for a peasant girl!

I was just about to explain this to the prince. But when I looked at him again, I thought better of it. His boots were caked with mud. He smelled like a horse. And when he took off his hat, his hair was a mess!

How disappointed Princess Aurora would be when she woke up and found her true love looking as if he'd been run over by a hay wagon, I thought. Wouldn't it be better for the young lovers to meet feeling clean and refreshed?

Against my better judgment, I did yet another good deed.

"I'm afraid your girlfriend has been delayed," I said. "In the meantime, would you like to join me for a cup of tea and a friendly chat at my office? You could tidy up while you're there."

Prince Phillip happily accepted my invitation. Leaving the cottage behind, I escorted him back to the Forbidden Mountains.

In no time at all, I had the prince comfortably settled in the "dungeon" (as we affectionately call our office lounge). Then, over a cozy cup of wormwood tea, I told him about the princess.

"I was just at King Stefan's castle," I explained. "And in the topmost tower Princess Aurora lies asleep, dreaming of her true love. But—you're never going to believe this—she is the same peasant maid who won your heart just yesterday!" By the time I'd finished explaining, I had tears in my eyes. It was such a touching story.

"It just proves true love conquers all," I said.

Of course, the prince was eager to see the princess as soon as possible. But—wouldn't you know it—at that very moment I received word of an emergency at work: three billy goats had caused a traffic jam on one of my troll bridges. Quickly setting down my cup, I told Prince Phillip I had some urgent business to attend to.

"Would you mind waiting for me here?" I asked. "I won't be long."

It's true that in my distraction, I may have accidentally locked Prince Phillip in the dungeon. But, dear me. There were plenty of employees around. All he had to do was knock on the door and someone would have let him out.

I swear, with simpletons like this in power, sometimes I fear for the future of our kingdom.

6

Trouble

Moments later, I was upstairs in my office when I heard a commotion down in the courtyard.

Looking out the window, I saw Prince Phillip galloping away on his horse. He dodged several arrows and narrowly missed a bath in boiling oil, poured from the parapet by my security guards.

"Dear me," I said to myself. "The prince must have forgotten his visitor's pass!"

I hurried out to the balcony to stop him. But there I received a horrible shock. My favorite pet raven was sitting on the railing . . . turned to stone!

That's when I noticed three familiar red, blue, and green shapes racing away with the prince—it was those nasty little fairies, Flora, Fauna, and Merryweather. Instantly I knew they were behind this vile prank.

Now, don't get me wrong. I can take a practical joke. But animal cruelty is no laughing matter! Those three fairies have always been jealous of my success. They were just looking for a chance to pull a stunt like this. Only this time they'd gone too far.

I intended to scold the fairies and give Prince Phillip a good talking-to. But when I finally caught up with them at King Stefan's castle, the sight before me filled me with alarm.

With a sword in one hand and a shield in the other, Prince Phillip was hacking away at the tangle of thorns and overgrown shrubbery around King Stefan's castle. (The king's gardeners are as lazy as his security guards.) At first I thought he was just pruning the hedges a bit. Then I caught sight of the crazed gleam in his eyes.

I knew then there could only be one explanation for the prince's odd behavior: those three nasty little fairies had cast a spell on him!

Those "good" fairies turned bad buzzed like hornets around the prince's head, whispering in his ear. No doubt about it, those pixies could stir up a lot of trouble!

Well, I called for help but every single soul in that fool palace seemed to be asleep. (It's a wonder that *anything* gets done in the kingdom at all!) It looked like it was up to me to put a stop to this tomfoolery before something—or someone—really got hurt.

I have since heard it rumored that I transformed myself into a fire-breathing dragon. I admit, I may not have been my usual charming self at that moment. I may have *snapped* at the prince a few times. But I certainly did not deserve what happened next.

Raising his sword, Prince Phillip heaved it with all his might. The sword sailed through the air, as if propelled by magic, and struck me in the chest. Luckily, I happened to be wearing an entire suit of chain mail beneath my dress (experience has taught me to never leave home without it). The sword bounced harmlessly away, tearing only my cloak, and I escaped down a steep ravine.

I count myself lucky to still be alive today. But I am sorry to say that my business did not get off so easily. After my encounter with the prince and those three bad fairies, some very hurtful gossip about me spread around the kingdom, and E.V.I.L. was forced to shut down. (The goose farm, the textile mills, and the troll bridges all were repossessed and sold to the highest bidder.) I'm hoping it's only a temporary situation.

In the meantime, however, life isn't so bad. Now that I'm not so busy, I have more time for charity work. Just last week I helped a sweet old woman do some repairs on her gingerbread house—a pair of young hooligans had eaten half of the roof! It's just scandalous how children behave these days.

Despite all my troubles, I have learned a valuable lesson. Although I loved being in charge of E.V.I.L., it was too big a job for just one person. Now I have a fourth rule of thumb: *What one can do well, two can do better*. For my next business venture, I've teamed up with some of my best friends. We have so many ideas: Big Bad Wolf Home Demolition, Captain Hook's Cruise Line, Jafar's Magic Carpet Import/Export. . . . I've realized the possibilities are endless when you work *together*.

Of course, I'll still be in charge. Some things never change.

GOING OUT
OF
BUSINESS
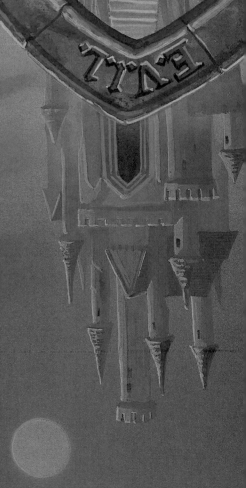
EVIL